Discover the DARK

Firespell

LOUISE COOPER

The Lost Brides

THERESA RADCLIFFE

DARK ENCHANTMENT

The Hounds of Winter

LOUISE COOPER

DARK ENCHANTMENT

Kiss of the Vampire

J. B. CALCHMAN

DARK ENCHANTMENT

Valley of Wolves

THERESA RADCLIFFE

DARK ENCHANTMENT

Blood Dance

LOUISE COOPER

Other titles in the DARK ENCHANTMENT series

BLOOD DANCE   Louise Cooper
DANCE WITH THE VAMPIRE   J. B. Calchman
FIRESPELL   Louise Cooper
THE HOUNDS OF WINTER   Louise Cooper
KISS OF THE VAMPIRE   J. B. Calchman
THE LOST BRIDES   Theresa Radcliffe
VALLEY OF WOLVES   Theresa Radcliffe

House of Thorns

JUDY DELAGHTY

PUFFIN BOOKS

PUFFIN BOOKS

Published by the Penguin Group
Penguin Books Ltd, 27 Wrights Lane, London w8 5tz, England
Penguin Books USA Inc., 375 Hudson Street, New York,
New York 10014, USA
Penguin Books Australia Ltd, Ringwood, Victoria, Australia
Penguin Books Canada Ltd, 10 Alcorn Avenue, Toronto, Ontario,
Canada m4v 3b2
Penguin Books (NZ) Ltd, 182–190 Wairau Road, Auckland 10,
New Zealand

Penguin Books Ltd, Registered Offices: Harmondsworth, Middlesex,
England

First published 1996
1 3 5 7 9 10 8 6 4 2

Filmset in 12/14 pt Monophoto Sabon
Typeset by Datix International Limited, Bungay, Suffolk
Made and printed in England by Clays Ltd, St Ives plc

CHAPTER I

ELAINE PRESSED HER face against the ancient glass of the window to get a better sight of the line of brightly painted caravans. The leaded panes made a diamond pattern on her cheek, and the glass was pleasantly cool in the hot summer afternoon.

'Do you see them, Gwen?' she asked.

Gwen turned from the tapestry she was working and looked at Elaine. 'I can't see anything much from here,' she said.

It was not the way a lady's maid ought to talk to her mistress, and she would have used a different voice if they had not been alone. But Elaine and Gwen had been brought up together, and felt themselves to be more like sisters than mistress and servant. Gwen, at sixteen, was just one year older than Elaine.

'Then come over here, you ape,' said Elaine.

Gwen pushed the needle into the cloth for safety and made her way to the window.

'See?' said Elaine.

'Oh, it's just the gypsies,' said Gwen, disappointed. 'I thought it was something important.'

'Aren't gypsies important enough for you?' asked Elaine. 'Nothing ever happens around here, does it? So we might as well make the most of this.'

'Raggle taggle rubbish,' said Gwen. 'They're all thieves and liars and frauds.'

'*He* doesn't look like raggle taggle rubbish,' said Elaine. She pointed to a young man, walking alongside the lead caravan. He was tall, and upright. His dark hair flowed back and his tread was firm and seemed to carry authority. A flash of silver glinted out from his head.

'Gypsy lovers aren't for the daughter of the Manor,' said Gwen.

Elaine pressed her face against the window again, glad to feel its cold flatness against her cheek.

The line of painted caravans twisted along the road through the parkland that surrounded the Manor House where she lived. It made its way down the slope, across the pasture and towards the river.

'They can't all be liars and thieves,' said Elaine at last.

Gwen paused, considered saying 'No, miss', then relented, and said instead, 'I think so.'

'Let's go and see,' said Elaine.

'What?' asked Gwen.

'I want some excitement,' said Elaine. 'I wish something would happen.'

'Be careful what you wish,' Gwen warned her. 'It might come true.'

'I wish it would,' said Elaine. 'I wish. I wish. I wish.'

Gwen frowned. 'Please,' she said. 'You never know what might happen.'

'No,' Elaine agreed. 'I don't know what will happen, but I'm going to find out.'

'How?' Gwen asked as she returned to the tapestry. 'How will you?' She looked at Elaine.

'From the gypsies,' said Elaine.

Gwen knew what the answer was going to be before she asked her next question, but she couldn't believe it. She wouldn't believe it. She denied it even as she asked. And she denied it loudly when Elaine answered. 'How will they know?' she made herself ask.

'Because I'm going to get them to tell my fortune,' said Elaine.

'No!' Gwen shouted. She surprised herself with the violence of her reaction, but she could not resist herself. Something in her chest seemed to grow tight and painful. 'No!' she repeated. 'You can't!'

'You'll remember who's mistress here, Miss Grey,' said Elaine.

Gwen bit her lip.

The gypsy caravans had arrived at the riverside, and they were drawing into a circle. Children ran around. Men built fires. Women tugged out blankets and rugs, and hung them on the boughs of trees to beat the dust of the road out of them.

Elaine looked out longingly at the busy scene, and wished herself there, in the fresh, warm air. She longed to wade into the water with the children, to tug off her stiff gown and to swim and splash about. Young ladies were not allowed near water. And an heiress was not taught to swim, but Elaine had never allowed that to stop her sneaking off and teaching herself. These days her time was always accounted for and her manners watched too carefully for such activities.

She put her hand to her tightly coiled hair, and she wished she could untie it, let it fall to her shoulders and be free. She looked across to Gwen, hoping to bring her into her dreams, but the needle went swiftly in and out of the fabric, and Gwen's lips were tight and her eyes half-closed in absent concentration.

Elaine's fingers undid her hair, almost without her thinking of what she was doing, or where she was.

Gwen, sneaking a look at her, noticed the lock fall to her shoulders. She sprang up and ran across the room. 'Look,' she said. 'Your hair.'

Elaine gave her a tricky smile. 'Are you going to pull it?' she asked. 'Or did you already, while I wasn't looking?'

Gwen drew herself up. 'You know very well I didn't,' she began.

Elaine hugged her. 'I'm sorry,' she said. 'Friends?'

Gwen softened. She smiled back at Elaine. 'Friends,' she agreed.

'So you'll come with me?' said Elaine. 'That's good.'

'Where?' Gwen was concentrating on a straying strand of Elaine's dark hair.

'To the gypsy camp. To have our fortunes told.'

'No,' said Gwen.

'But something's got to happen. It must. I know it must.' Elaine squeezed Gwen's arm. 'To tell you the truth, Gwen, I can feel it. I know that something's going to happen. I have to go to the gypsy to find out what it is.'

'If we get caught,' said Gwen, 'you'll be in trouble. You'll be watched all the time, kept to your room, forbidden to leave the house.'

'Yes,' agreed Elaine.

'But it will be worse for me. I'll be sent away from the house. I'll have nowhere to go, nothing to live on. Instead of this gown, and a comfortable bed, and meals every day, I'll be homeless and penniless.'

Elaine's face fell.

Gwen's father had died in battle before she was born. Her mother had died as Gwen was born. Gwen had been an orphan before she had finished screaming her way into the world. Elaine's mother had taken her in out of pity. Gwen had no other home, no other family.

'Then I'll go alone,' said Elaine. 'I'm sorry I asked you. It was wrong of me.'

Gwen finished Elaine's hair in silence.

A creak on the landing told them that someone was about to arrive.

'Quick,' said Gwen.

Elaine rushed over to the tapestry, grabbed the needle and pretended to sew. Gwen began to tidy the combs and brushes away, as a maid should.

'Come,' said Elaine quietly, in response to the respectful knock.

The door opened.

'Miss Elaine,' said a footman. 'You are called to the Great Hall.' He closed the door.

They looked at each other in wonder.

'What?' asked Elaine.

Gwen spread her hands in helpless silence.

'They only ever use the Great Hall for business,' said Elaine. 'Important business.'

'So why should they want a woman there?' said Gwen, with a bitterness that even surprised herself.

'Come with me,' said Elaine. 'I'm afraid.'

'I'm not summoned,' said Gwen. 'They won't let me in.'

'I need you there. Hide behind the arras.'

It was an old hiding-place. They had often stood together behind the thick brocade curtain. The Great Hall was a place of secrets – adult secrets – men's secrets. So they had made sure, when they were children, that they should find out what those secrets were. Mostly they were boring secrets. Rent collecting from the tenants. Wills signed in front of witnesses and attorneys.

Once, only once, the secret had been exciting. Elaine's father, as Lord of the Manor and Magistrate, had held a court and tried a man for stealing a loaf of bread. The punishment was death, usually. But this time the thief was allowed off with only a beating. Gwen and Elaine still remembered the pitiful gratitude the man had shown, and the tears of joy his wife had shed. But they also remembered the savage flogging he had received, the blood on his back . . . and the screams. They had not gone back to the Great Hall after that.

So Gwen hid behind the arras when Elaine stepped into the Great Hall and saw her father and mother, and the attorney who made out their wills, and the three strangers, with the fair hair and pale skins, who stood by, waiting with them.

'Ah, Elaine,' said her father, and he put out his arms to welcome her. 'This is the most important day of your life.'

CHAPTER II

ELAINE STEPPED FORWARD and greeted her father. The attorney nodded approvingly at the way she curtsied low to her father.

Elaine remembered him from those other days. She remembered his thin face, white hair, pinched mouth and reedy voice. She remembered that day, when the bread thief had been tried, how the attorney had urged that the man should be hanged for the theft. And she remembered how her father had mentioned the man's poverty, his starving wife and children. She remembered how the attorney had made it clear that not to punish at all would bring down the reputation of the law in that county and her father's reputation as a just magistrate. She remembered the pleasure he had shown, when the lash fell on the thief's back.

While remembering all this, and her hatred for the attorney, she remembered too her years of training in manners, and she smiled at him, and curtsied.

'Elaine,' said her father, 'I want you to meet some friends.'

'Whose friends?' she asked.

He frowned, but chose to ignore the rudeness of the question. 'This is Peter,' he said, indicating a young man. 'And his father. And this is their attorney.'

'Two men of law at one time,' said Elaine. 'A rare privilege.'

Peter put out his hand to greet Elaine. She looked at him closely. He was taller than she was, taller than her father even. And his fair hair hung in soft curves round a handsome face.

Elaine gave him her hand. He smiled and took it warmly.

Elaine's father and mother looked at each other and smiled.

Elaine's mouth did not move.

Peter gripped her hand firmly and touched her elbow with his other hand. Elaine flinched.

'I am pleased to meet you,' said Peter. His voice was strong, yet not harsh.

Elaine looked at him coolly. He was tall, handsome, well mannered, with a good smile and a strong hand. He spoke clearly, and with patient interest.

She hated him, instantly.

Why?

What was it about this person that made her flesh crawl and her hair prickle on her head?

Elaine forced herself to reply, but she could not say what he had said, that she was pleased to meet him. She would not lie to him. Something told her that she must not give any sign or indication that she was pleased. Somehow she felt that it was a trap she must not fall into.

'I hope that my father has made you welcome,' she said. Elaine congratulated herself on her diplomacy.

'Your father is the best host in the world,' said Peter, 'but I hope that you will welcome me too, after all this time.'

It was as though he had seen straight through her, and knew her feelings. She turned her head away.

'See,' said Peter's father. 'You have made her blush, Peter.'

Elaine clenched her fist, hidden in her gown. She was angry with them all. Angry with Peter for his challenge. Angry with his father for his accusation. But most of all she was angry with her own father. Why had he brought her here to meet a passing stranger? 'I do not understand you. What do you mean, *after all this time*? Have we met before?'

Peter smiled. 'We have not met,' he said. 'But our families have long memories of each other.'

Peter's father looked solemn. 'And not always happy ones,' he added.

Elaine breathed deeply. Her chest felt tight and painful. She knew what was going to be said next. Suddenly she knew. And she wanted to be wrong.

'Peter is the Heir of Thorncliffe,' her father said. 'And his father is the Lord of Thorncliffe.'

It was as though the Devil himself had been welcomed into their Great Hall. Thorncliffe was a place of fear and danger to Elaine. As a child she had been warned that if she was naughty she would be sent there one day. And the Heir of Thorncliffe was the bogey man who would carry her away. The families had hated each other time out of mind.

'A time must come for peace. That time is now. We must transact our business,' said her father. 'And then we can eat.'

Elaine curtsied again, said, 'I hope you enjoy your stay with us, and that you have a safe journey home.' It was the nearest she could come to saying that she wished them on their way as swiftly as possible. Then she began to turn to leave the Great Hall.

Her father laughed. 'Not so fast.'

Elaine hesitated, then turned back to him.

'You must stay for our business,' he said. 'After all, it is your business most of all. And you are no longer a child.'

The two attorneys sat at a table and exchanged documents. The stiff parchment crackled as it was passed from hand to hand.

More deeds. But she could not understand why she had been summoned. They could end their feud without her there to watch. How stupid grown-ups were.

The documents were examined by everyone except Elaine and her mother. When all the men had approved them, they took ink and pens and signed them, Peter's father first, then Peter, then her own father. Finally, the two attorneys signed them.

Elaine's mother squeezed her hand and looked at her with soft eyes.

Elaine waited for her turn to sign, but the ink was dried on the parchment, the pens taken away by a servant, and the papers exchanged and put into leather folders without her signature being required.

'Am I not to sign?' she asked.

Her father frowned.

'That isn't necessary,' he said.

'Besides,' her mother added, 'you are not of age to sign a legal paper, and even if you were, then a woman's signature would not count. I did not sign either.'

Elaine stood up. 'Then I wonder that you bothered to bring me here at all.'

The Lord of Thorncliffe laughed, and said to Elaine's father, 'You were right, sir, she has spirit and a strong will.' The men laughed together. Then he said to Peter, 'It will be lifetime's work to tame her, Peter.'

'Less time than that, I hope,' he replied.

Elaine gasped. She was furious that she should be spoken about as though she were not there. And she was astonished to be spoken of in this way, like a horse or a dog. But most of all she began to feel more afraid than ever. And at last she began to understand what was happening and why she had been summoned to the Great Hall.

Peter took a small leather box from his pocket and opened it. A bright silver bracelet nestled in folds of velvet. It was ornate and complicated. Briar twigs tangled together, with sharp thorns. It was beautiful, but dangerous. He held it out to Elaine.

She faced her father and demanded, 'What is happening here? Why is this –' she hesitated, looked at the handsome young man, then spat out the word, 'this *creature* speaking of me like this?'

Her father controlled his anger, but Elaine recognized the furious expression on his face and the slow, deliberate way he spoke when he was in a rage.

'I am disappointed, Elaine, that you should appear like this, especially on such a day as today, and before such guests.'

'What day, Father? Tell me. I do not like these men and I do not trust them. You should not have let them come here. No good will come of it, I warn you. They are Thorncliffes and they are our enemies.'

This was too much for her father and his fury exploded. 'Take the bridal gift from him.'

Elaine set her face like flint. 'Never,' she said.

The attorney watched with interest. His thin face seemed to be amused at the scene, and his cruel fingers twitched on the leather folder.

'Sir,' said Peter. 'Please do not ask it for me.' He still held the box.

'Not for you,' Elaine's father said, 'for me. For my family. For Elaine herself.'

Elaine said, 'I will never marry Peter Thorncliffe. Ever. You have no right to dispose of me in this way.'

Her father put out his hand and the attorney gave him the folder. He took out the parchment, and showed it to Elaine. 'Here is one copy. The other is with Thorncliffe's attorney. You saw it signed. You saw it sealed. You smelt the hot wax and watched the signet impress it. Before this year is out, you will be the wife of the Heir of Thorncliffe. It is written. Our feud is over.' He handed the folder back.

Peter's lips seemed to Elaine to move in a half-smile of triumph. And then, in that instant, she knew why she had hated the young man on first sight. He had come to buy her, to take her away, to own her – with or without her consent or her approval, or her love. She was no more than a piece of property to him. She spoke calmly. 'I said *never*. And never it will be. I will see my future in another place.'

This was too much for her father. 'Go,' he roared. 'Now!'

'I will go,' she said. 'But because I choose to go, not because I am ordered to.'

The apologies for her behaviour filled her ears and made her burn with shame as she left the Hall.

CHAPTER III

G WEN WAS ALREADY in the room when
Elaine returned. The back steps and pas-
sageways were quicker than the wide
staircase that Elaine used. She did not look at
Elaine.

'You heard everything?'

'Yes,' said Gwen. She picked up her needle
again.

'I will never marry the Heir of Thorncliffe,'
said Elaine.

Gwen answered quietly. 'I think you will
have to.'

'No! I won't be the wife of that blond fool.'

Gwen carried on sewing as she said, 'I told
you that if we should be caught doing wrong,
then you would be kept here, and I would be
sent away. Now it is all different. Now there is
somewhere to send you. And you will be sent.
You must marry him. There is no choice. They
will not let you stay here.'

'I won't!'

Gwen's silence brought back Elaine's rage.
She knew that Gwen believed that the marriage
would go ahead, and that Elaine knew it
too and was only arguing and fighting
helplessly.

'I can prove it,' said Elaine. 'I won't marry him. I can prove it. Do you believe me?'

Faced with a direct challenge, Gwen had to answer. 'No,' she said.

'Challenge me.'

'All right.'

'You'll come and let me prove it?'

'Yes,' Gwen agreed.

'Promise,' demanded Elaine.

'Promise.'

'We'll do it tonight.'

'How?' Gwen looked puzzled.

'We'll go to the gypsy camp. I'll have my fortune told. Then you'll see. It won't be Peter Thorncliffe I'll marry.'

The years slipped away and Elaine and Gwen felt like small girls again. The sun was setting behind the trees, casting a glowing orange light in the room. From downstairs the noise of preparations drifted up. Servants hurried with great dishes. Small boys polished silver until their arms ached. The glass shone on the broad tables. The wine was poured into huge jugs. Women arranged huge sprays of fresh flowers on sideboards and serving tables. The Feast was on its way.

Elaine and Gwen sat side by side on the bed, their feet drawn up beneath them. Elaine's mother sat near to them, on a chair, as though she were planning to tell them a bedtime story.

And it was a story.

But it was no fairy tale, no magical tale of witches and goblins and happy endings. It was the only story there could ever be for Elaine. It was her past and it was her future. And she looked on with a set face and staring eyes.

'This story is older than anyone can tell,' said her mother. 'From a time before books were written, or maps were drawn; from a time before there were wills and deeds and attorneys.'

'That must have been a good time,' said Elaine.

'It was a time when the Thorncliffes and the Wolds were friends,' her mother continued. 'The Lord of Thorncliffe and the Lord of the Wolds hunted together. They shared horses and hawks. They even looked alike. People would mistake them for one another. Dark and tall and slim.'

'But Peter Thorncliffe and his father are fair,' said Elaine.

'Wait,' said her mother. 'They made visits and planned feasts. But they did not marry.'

'Why?' asked Elaine.

'Because they needed each other too much.'

'I don't understand.'

'Each estate could only help the other in time of need if they were separate. By uniting they would be as one. And if disaster struck, then they would both fall. They signed an agreement.'

'It need not be like that,' said Elaine.

'Perhaps. But that was what they had decided. No marriage between a Thorncliffe and a Wold.'

'So it should always be,' said Elaine.

'Please,' said Gwen. 'What happened? What changed it?'

Elaine's mother smiled. 'You always were quicker than Elaine,' she said. 'What always happens? Someone fell in love. They tried to stop it. But you never can.'

'Who?' said Elaine. 'Who was it?'

'It was the Heir of Thorncliffe. His name was Mikal, and he fell in love with the Daughter of the Wolds.'

'Go on.'

'She loved him, too, and they asked permission to marry. But it was impossible. The agreement was binding in law. There was no way out of it.'

'What did they do?' Gwen asked.

'He was sent away, for a year. To think about it. He believed that if he still wanted to marry after that, then he would be allowed to. But while he was away, a marriage was arranged between her and another person.'

'No!' said Elaine. 'That's wrong. You can't arrange marriages.'

She stared at her mother.

'I agree,' said the older woman, quietly. 'Which is why I am here tonight. To warn you.'

'I don't have to marry him?' said Elaine.

'She refused. The date was set. The contract was signed. The day arrived. They went to wake her, on her wedding day . . .' Her voice trembled. She could not go on.

'Did she marry him?' Elaine demanded impatiently.

'She was dead.'

'No. How?'

'Poison. She had killed herself.'

'You see,' said Elaine. 'You see. You can't make someone.'

'It's only a story,' said her mother. 'It probably never happened like that.'

'I'll kill myself,' said Elaine. 'I will. If you make me marry him.'

'Will you?' Her mother searched Elaine's face. 'Will you? Your father says you won't.'

Elaine turned away. 'Yes, I will,' she said.

'When the girl died, our ancestors demanded a terrible revenge. They insisted that Mikal should die as well. He was made to swallow poison.'

'It was wrong. One death was enough,' said Elaine. Her eyes were blazing and she was flushed with anger.

'One was too many,' said Gwen.

Elaine's mother looked at her gratefully. 'And another won't help,' she added. 'So the old agreement was changed. And now it was made that the Thorncliffes and Wolds could never help each other until the evil had been undone and the two heirs married each other.

The feud was too bitter. They have not met for years, not talked for generations. Until now. Now there are two heirs, you and Peter.'

'Never,' said Elaine.

'Then we will all be ruined.'

'Better that than marry him.'

'I think, in the end, you will have no choice.'

'Change the agreement.'

'We tried. The attorneys say there is no way.'

'Then I'll poison myself,' said Elaine.

'I hope not,' said her mother. 'And I believe you won't.'

'Why?'

'You said it yourself. One death is enough.'

Elaine looked away.

'And now,' said her mother, rising, 'I must prepare myself for the Feast. And so must you.'

'And that's why they are blond?' asked Gwen.

'Yes. They married a family from the north. They have been fair ever since.' Elaine's mother produced a leather box, opened it and revealed the thorn bracelet. 'Wear this to the Feast,' she said. 'It is the betrothal band.'

'No,' said Elaine. 'I'll throw it out of the window.'

Her mother sighed and took it back. 'I won't leave it, then. Not now. Do not disgrace us at the Feast.'

Elaine longed to run across and bury her face in her mother's skirts and ask her to make it all right. But she knew that this time it was too late.

CHAPTER IV

THE FEAST WAS over. The window was black with the night sky, except where the diamond panes caught the light of stars and threw it into the room.

Elaine pulled on a cloak and hugged it to herself. Although the summer night was warm, she shivered and she needed the comfort of the thick folds of cloth. 'Did you see him at dinner tonight?' she asked.

'I was surprised you were allowed to go to dinner,' said Gwen.

'Hah! You were here. You heard. I was *made* to go, not allowed to go. I wouldn't go near him if I had a choice. He couldn't take his eyes off me. Every time I looked up he was looking at me, as though he owned me. Like a farmer with a new horse.'

'Perhaps he's fallen in love with you,' said Gwen. 'Perhaps he likes looking at you.' She took Elaine's hand. 'May I speak?'

Elaine hugged her. 'Of course. Why do you ask?'

'Well,' Gwen said. 'He is young and handsome.'

'So?'

'And he is the heir to a great estate.'

'None of that means anything to me.'

'It would be a home.'

'Home?' Elaine gave a mocking laugh. 'What sort of home would Thorncliffe be? A great, glowering manor, with bars at the windows and dark, dank cellars, where the rats run and the toads squat. The gardens run wild and full of thorns. Remember? Thorncliffe is the home of thorns and they creep and twist and lie. And the Lords of Thorncliffe creep and twist and lie, as well. Remember?'

Gwen remembered it all too well. The bedtime stories. The warnings. The wagged finger and the shaken head. 'The Heir of Thorncliffe will carry you off, to Thorncliffe Hall, where the toads squat.' And all the rest of it. Gwen remembered it as well as Elaine did. 'He could be none of those things,' she said.

'Except rich,' said Elaine.

'He could be old.'

'Or ugly,' said Elaine.

Gwen took a bigger risk. 'Or both,' she whispered.

She giggled. And Elaine joined in. And they were girls again, not young women. Girls looking at the grooms and deciding which one was really a prince in disguise, which one they would like to marry.

'You can have him,' said Elaine.

Gwen punched her softly. 'That wouldn't work,' she said. And they giggled more.

'Shh,' Elaine warned. 'They'll hear us.'

Suddenly she was serious again. 'I've caught you,' she said.

'What?' Gwen was startled.

'You're trying to persuade me to marry him,' said Elaine. 'Hush, it's all right. Don't protest. I don't mind. But it means you weren't telling the truth.'

'When?'

'When you said I would marry him. You think I might not. Don't you?'

'I'm sorry, Elaine I think you'll do what the contract says.'

'So we have to go to the gypsy camp. We *have* to.'

The men were still talking inside when Gwen and Elaine crept across the lawn, over the parkland and down towards the river.

Elaine was wrapped in her hooded cloak. Gwen walked openly in her gown, with a light cape over her shoulders. A hedgehog scuttled away from them in alarm.

'Careful, urchin,' said Gwen, 'they'll pop you in the pot.'

'Gwen,' protested Elaine. 'Don't say that.'

'It's true, though,' said Gwen. 'They eat them. In stews.'

'No, we don't,' said a voice.

Gwen and Elaine spun round. There was figure in the shadow of the trees.

'Who are you?' Elaine asked.

'We don't put them in stews,' he repeated.

Gwen looked defiant. 'I've heard you do,' she said.

'Shh, Gwen,' said Elaine. 'They don't eat them.'

'Oh, we eat them,' he said. 'We bake them in clay and then pull off the spines and skin when they're cooked. But we don't put them in stews.'

'You're disgusting,' said Gwen.

'Yes. Remember that,' he said. There was a rustle, and he was gone.

'Who are you?' Elaine leaped forward and searched for him. But there was no more sign of him than if he had been a whiff of smoke.

'Let's go back,' said Gwen. 'It's dangerous.'

'No, we're going there.'

'It's dangerous. They don't want us. They're mocking us.'

'You can go back if you want,' said Elaine.

Gwen followed her reluctantly, but she looked around, fearful of who might step out of the shadows next.

The smell of cooking was mingled with smoke from the fires, and with something else, something richer, deeper, more fragrant and mysterious. Gwen hung back, but Elaine pressed on.

She broke through the ring of caravans to where the dry earth had been beaten flat and hard. Hesitantly, she and Gwen kept in the shadow of a caravan and watched. Groups of gypsies sat eating, talking, drinking and playing with children.

There was a large fire in the centre of the ring and several smaller, family fires near to caravans. A cooking pot hung over the central fire. People went over and ladled some sort of stew out of it from time to time, and carried it back to their groups. No one seemed to watch over it.

Gwen pinched Elaine. 'That looks disgusting,' she said.

'It smells good,' said Elaine, 'and at least we know it isn't hedgehog.'

'It might be something worse,' said Gwen.

Their whispers attracted attention.

Someone spoke sharply in a foreign language, and there was a quick movement of light and the two young women found themselves standing in the glow of a blazing torch and with all eyes in the circle turned on them. A low, threatening mumble grew in intensity.

'We should run,' said Gwen. Rough hands pulled them forward, into the circle.

Gwen struggled back, but Elaine shrugged herself free and stepped forward boldly. 'You are welcome,' she said.

The murmuring stopped, then rose in an angry babble.

'Silence!' a squat old man, with a hunched back, shouted, and the noise ceased instantly. 'Thank you,' he said, 'but who are you to bid us welcome?'

'My father is the Lord of the Manor,' said Elaine. 'I am Elaine of the Wolds, and you are resting on our land. In his name I welcome you.'

'This is our land,' the old gypsy said. 'Nevertheless I thank you just the same.'

'No,' said Elaine. 'Our land goes right down to the river bank, and for miles on the other side. It has been so for as long as any can remember. We hold the title deeds. It is ours by law. You are wrong.'

The murmuring began again, but the old man held up his hand and it stopped. 'You are right,' he agreed. 'But wrong, too. We have been travelling here for generations, longer than anyone can remember – before there were title deeds to Paradise. Your law does not affect us. Where we stop is ours, until we move on. And then we give it back for a time, until we return. And while we stop, then all who visit us follow *our* laws.'

Elaine sensed a power and authority about the man that she had not expected to find, and she was taken aback. Something of her confusion showed on her face, for the man nodded, and said, 'You expected perhaps barbarians, ignorant people, with no laws, no leaders. I am sorry to disappoint you. But do not be afraid –'

'I'm not afraid,' snapped Elaine.

'No,' the gypsy said, 'I do not think you are. Good. Well, I bid you welcome, with the same generosity you offered to us, though it was not yours to give.' There was a low rumble of approval from the figures gathered round. 'You must eat,' he said.

'No,' said Gwen, too quickly.

The man laughed. 'It is good meat,' he said.

'Thank you,' said Elaine. 'We have eaten already. But I do come with a request.'

All eyes were turned on her with intense curiosity.

'Say it,' the old man invited her.

Elaine did not like to speak in front of the crowd. And then she was afraid of what the gypsy fortune-teller would say to her. And, even more frightening, there was the image of an old hag in her caravan, who would cackle at her and put Elaine's soft hand in her hard claw and read her palm.

'No, miss,' Gwen warned her. 'We should go back to the Manor.'

'Yes,' agreed Elaine. 'Another time. We will return tomorrow, perhaps.'

'Or the next day,' said Gwen.

A mocking laugh went up, led by a voice that they recognized. The voice from the shadows.

'It must be tonight,' said another voice, a gentle voice. 'It must be now.'

The huddle of faces pressing in on Elaine fell back, and she saw the darkness of the night above the fire. 'What?' she demanded.

'You come for your fortune?' It was both a question and a statement.

'Don't answer,' said Gwen.

'Yes,' said Elaine.

'Very well, it shall be told. But not tomorrow. Not later. Tonight. Now.'

Elaine cast her eyes about, seeking to find the person who belonged to the voice, but she could not.

'No!' It was the voice from the shadows again. 'You must not.' Elaine saw at last who this voice belonged to. It was a young man. Not so tall as Peter, but taller than herself. But he was as dark as Peter was fair. His hair was shiny and gathered back with an intricate silver clip into a tail that swept his collar. He stood straight and strong. Elaine recognized him as the figure who had led the caravans, striding confidently over what she had then thought of as her father's land, and now was not so sure. His face was lean, and his bright eyes reminded her of a fox she had once reared when its mother had been killed in a trap. He had the same sharp intelligence; the same alertness; the same wild nature. She wished she could reach out and touch him, stroke him, as she had the fox. He might snap, but he might not. He might let her touch something of the wildness in himself and make it hers.

'Must not?'

'Not for an outsider. You must not receive an outsider. It will bring ill luck.'

'I think not, Cam,' said the gentle voice. 'There is always room here for an outsider. For a time.'

'No,' Cam insisted.

Elaine felt herself begin to dislike him, to fear the wildness, and this turned to anger and stubbornness. 'I will go,' she said. 'Now, to hear my fortune.'

The faces smiled. The voices murmured approval.

'Send her to the Tent of Prophecy,' said the gentle voice.

Gwen kept close to Elaine and began to follow her. She was held back, kindly, yet firmly.

'Those who go to the Tent of Prophecy, go alone,' said the old man. 'Stay and eat.'

A laugh went up and a ladle clattered into a bowl. Gwen sat by the fire.

Elaine was hurried forward until she found herself at the foot of some wooden steps that disappeared into a caravan. Looking up she saw that its wooden sides were painted with strange symbols and signs, with unnatural beasts and grotesque monsters.

'Enter,' said a voice from inside the caravan.

CHAPTER V

Elaine's head was swimming as she stepped inside the gaudy caravan. Her eyes were blurred with fear and she could not take anything in, but she kept her head high, trying to hide her terror. She wanted to turn and run, straight back to her father, to safety, but her pride was stronger than her fear, and her father had betrayed her. And an image of Peter Thorncliffe swam before her eyes, and she knew that there was no safety for her at home any more. She might as well go forward as look back.

'Sit.' It was the same gentle voice that Elaine had heard outside. Something in the voice soothed her fears enough for her to be able to look around and see where she was.

The walls of the caravan were spread with deeply coloured hangings. The floor was soft and warm, covered with a Turkish carpet. These were brought to mysterious light by the glow from several ornate lamps. The air was scented with incense from a small brass burner that hung from a delicate chain. And this fragrance was mixed with something else, more elusive and alluring, a perfume that belonged, not to a place, but to a person. Elaine knew that it came from the figure who was seated at the small round table in the centre of the caravan.

She obeyed the voice and sat.

The figure kept her head down, her face concealed by the folds of dark, patterned muslin that covered it.

When Elaine was frightened or nervous she often attacked, and she did so now. 'This isn't a tent,' she said.

'No?'

'Then why do they call it the Tent of Prophecy?' It made her feel better to take control.

'Does it look like a tent?' the woman asked.

'No,' said Elaine.

'Look around you.'

'Yes,' said Elaine. 'It does inside.'

The hanging folds and the rich colours gave a soft, flowing line to the sides of the caravan, so much so that it seemed to Elaine for a moment as though she were in a tent. 'It's just hangings,' she said, uncertainly.

'Yes?'

'You can make anywhere look like anything,' Elaine said.

'We lived in tents long before we had caravans,' said the woman. 'Prophecy needs a tent.'

Elaine had a feeling that if she tried to walk out she would find that her feet touched sand and her eyes would see desert stars. There would be no circle of caravans, no people, no fire. Just a lone tent in the darkness.

The woman half lifted her head, so that

Elaine could see her forehead and her eyes. She shuddered and knew that somehow the inside and the outside were not the same, that she was alone, far from Gwen and from home. She searched the woman's eyes, afraid of what she would see there. 'I've brought money for you,' she said, her voice shaking.

Now that the moment had come she was terrified.

The old woman nodded. 'Silver?'

'Yes.'

Elaine opened a leather purse and poured some coins on the table. They made a dull ring against the cloth. To her surprise, the woman took one, slipped it into her robe and pushed the others back.

'They're all for you,' said Elaine.

'I take only what is right,' the woman said.

Elaine fumbled the other coins back into the purse, aware all the time of the woman's eyes on her, that she was being judged, assessed.

'Give me your hand.'

The moment Elaine had dreaded had at last arrived. She would have to let the gypsy woman touch her. The thought made her tremble. And she would at the same time put herself in her power, allow her to look right into her heart and life. There were things that even Gwen did not know. Secrets about herself that Elaine would die rather than tell. And this woman might see them, bring them into the dull light of the Tent of Prophecy. It was too much, too frightening.

Slowly, Elaine put her hand on to the table, closed her eyes and waited. She felt the sleeve of the woman's robe brush against her wrist. She drew in her breath sharply, then relaxed. The hand that took hers were soft and dry.

Elaine felt one hand beneath hers, holding her still, the other opened her fingers with delicate care. Her eyelids grew heavier still, and, if she had wanted to open them and look at the woman, she felt she could not. But she was happy to let the gypsy hold her hand and look deep into her, happy to keep her eyes closed and drift with the sensation of giving herself up to whatever was about to happen.

'I see a man in your hand,' said the woman.

Elaine waited. It was the usual gypsy nonsense.

The soft hands stroked her palm, making her tingle.

'See him,' said the woman. 'See the man I see.'

Elaine let the darkness beneath her eyelids lift and clear, allowed pictures to form. A tall figure walked towards her. His hand was open, and he reached out to her. Elaine gasped and opened her eyes.

'No,' said the woman. 'Rest. Close your eyes. Wait.'

Elaine saw the veil, the dark eyes, the clear forehead. She smelled the fragrance of the musk the woman wore. She longed to trust her, to give herself into this woman's power. But she held back.

'See him,' said the woman. 'Close your eyes. He is there.'

He stood in front of a huge old house. The sun was rising, just above the chimneys, and it dazzled Elaine as she looked at him. He was tall, powerful, and his hair hung round his shoulders.

Elaine wanted to open her eyes again, to feel safe, to be out of this vision. Yet she needed to see who he was. She desperately wanted it not to be Peter. But he was tall, like Peter. And he stood with an air of confidence, almost arrogance, just as Peter had done in the Great Hall. Again he put out his hand, beckoned her forward.

Elaine held back, but she wanted so much to go forward, to reach out and take his hand. He drew her to him, and she could not resist. She screwed up her eyes, as though squinting into the sun, trying to cut out the glare and to see him clearly.

The sun rose above the house. The roof, chimneys and walls were black against its brightness, and the tall figure grew ever more indistinct.

'Who are you?' Elaine called out. She meant to speak silently, in the vision, to the young man, but her voice rang out in the caravan and disappeared into the folds of rich fabric.

Her eyes opened suddenly, and she looked

around, startled, uncertain for a moment where she was.

The old woman's eyes penetrated Elaine. They pierced her and laid bare her thoughts. 'You saw him?'

'Yes,' Elaine whispered.

'Do you want him?'

'I don't know. Who is he?' Elaine was trembling. Her voice was shaky.

'You did not recognize him, then? He is a stranger?'

'I don't know. He stood against the light. I saw, but I didn't see him. Not his face. Not clearly. Not at all, really.'

The old woman nodded. Her veil slipped a little and she reached up and adjusted it to hide her.

'May I see you?' Elaine asked.

'Not yet.'

'Before I go?'

'Perhaps.'

'Who did I see?'

'I saw nothing,' said the woman. 'The sight is yours, not mine.' She looked at Elaine, as though waiting for her to say something else.

Elaine breathed in the incense. She still felt relaxed and sleepy, not at all nervous any more. A sudden loud roar of laughter, followed by applause, broke outside.

Elaine turned her head, though the door to the caravan was closed. There was a muffled noise on the steps. Something like a large animal – a dog, or . . .

Elaine returned to concentrating on the woman sitting opposite her, preferring not to imagine what animal might be lurking outside.

The woman still waited, silently.

'I think I did know who I saw,' said Elaine.

'Yes?'

'I can't be sure . . .'

The woman sat silently, expectantly.

'There was something about the way he stood, about his height. I don't know. I didn't really recognize him, but I know I've seen him before. Can't you tell me more?' Elaine said.

'Of course,' said the woman.

Elaine felt the anger welling up in her. 'You said you couldn't.'

'No.'

'You *did*. You said you couldn't see him. Only I could see him.'

'Yes. Only you. But there are other ways.'

'Then why didn't you tell me?' Elaine demanded.

'You must ask,' said the woman. 'You must always ask. It is the way we do things here. Nothing is offered, except food and shelter. The rest, well . . .' She paused.

'What?' said Elaine.

'The rest is dangerous. It must be not offered. You must always ask. Perhaps you do not want to know.'

'I do,' said Elaine. 'I must. Please, tell me who it was I saw. You can?'

'Oh, yes. I can tell you. But are you sure you want to know?'

'*Yes*. Tell me. Please. Please tell me.'

CHAPTER VI

GWEN SWALLOWED. THE food was rich and spicy. It made her blink with surprise. She put the spoon to her mouth quickly to take some more before she should forget the taste. A cheer went up round the fire and Gwen dropped her head. The spices were delicate and subtle, not hot and fierce. She moved the food around, trying to explore everything about it, letting her tongue enjoy the texture and the warmth of the meat. She swallowed again, and felt her head grow light.

'She's like all the rest,' said a cynical voice.

The spell of the food was broken for a moment. Gwen looked up. The young man stood between her and the fire. She saw his powerful frame against the light.

'Cam,' said the old man, 'she is our guest.'

'That isn't the point,' the young man said. 'The point is they hate us because they won't trust us, won't get to know us. They think we're thieves and liars and frauds.'

Gwen was shocked to hear Cam use the very words she had spoken to Elaine when the caravans had arrived. It was as though he had been in the room with them, hidden, listening.

'You've been spying on us,' she said, before she could think of what her words meant.

'See,' he said. 'See? She admits it.'

'Go,' said the old man. 'Leave us until you are in better temper, till you can be courteous to our visitor.'

Cam gave the man a look that made Gwen gasp with fear. It was an anger stronger than anything she had ever known. He turned and walked off.

'I am sorry. Please, eat.'

Gwen watched the broad shoulders and straight back of Cam as he stalked off into the darkness. She filled her mouth again, and gave herself over to pleasure, enjoying the mysterious effects of the food.

Cam made his way deliberately, like a hunter.

The lamps in the Tent of Prophecy cast ghostly shadows. The table between Elaine and the gypsy woman was scattered with ancient parchments and plans.

'Maps,' said the gypsy. 'Choose one.'

Elaine considered them. She had seen plans of the estate before. Dusty documents, lawyers' business. She had no interest in them. There were documents like that here. But there were others as well. There were maps, blue-painted, with tiny dots of islands in a calm sea. Whales spouted and mermaids swam through deep oceans. Elaine wanted to take one of these. She wanted the gypsy to tell her that she would go to sea, leave her home, her family, and that she would never marry, ever.

But she held her hand back, and it felt as though she could not escape that way. She laid the sea chart aside and looked at the others.

The gypsy woman watched her. 'Not the sea?' she asked.

'Is that the one?' asked Elaine, a sudden surge of hope leaping in her.

'Only you can tell.'

'I want it to be.'

'Then, take it.'

'It doesn't feel right.'

'Then leave it be,' the woman advised.

'But am I learning my future or am I making it?' asked Elaine.

The woman looked at her, and Elaine felt that there was at last something more in the eyes, something of approval in the hidden face. She needed to know. 'Please,' she said. 'May I see who you are?'

'Yes,' said the woman. 'Yes. But only when you have chosen.'

'What am I to choose?' Elaine asked.

'You came to know the future,' said the woman.

Elaine asked her the same question again. 'Will I learn it, or will I make it?'

'That is up to you.'

'Then,' said Elaine, 'I will make it.' She seized a map that had been tantalizing her and swept the others away. 'This one,' she said.

It was old, very old. The edges were worn thin and ragged. Most of it was green and brown, thick forest. Blue rivers meandered through the trees. A lake filled one corner. By the lake stood a great house, dark and forbidding. There was a village, huddled in a clearing. But it was not these that attracted Elaine. A city began on the east side of the map and fell off the edge. A city of towers and spires, winding streets and narrow alleys. A city of gardens and courtyards and fountains. Elaine wanted to go there, and to walk along the street that led to the edge of the map, and then on, into new and uncharted areas.

In the wild part, Elaine's eyes saw what she was almost sure was not true: dragons in caves to the south of the lake; a beast, half-hidden in the water. A monster with yellow eyes crouched at the door of the great house. It was a magical land, a land far away from Elaine's world.

The look of approval in the woman's eyes flickered, then they became blank. 'Be very sure,' she warned.

Elaine hesitated, then pushed the map forward. 'This one.'

The gypsy smoothed the map on the table. She took the silver coin that Elaine had given to her and handed it back. 'Spin it,' she said.

Elaine flipped the coin.

'No,' said the woman. 'Like this.' She put the coin on its rim, on the map, and spun it, taking care to grab it before it could come to rest.

Elaine copied her. She put the coin on the city and spun it.

The coin, instead of slowing down, spun faster and faster. Elaine waited for it to stop. It gleamed in the light and threw beams of silver on to the walls. It hummed, and danced. Elaine watched it, becoming anxious as it moved away from the city. The coin travelled slowly across the map, now here, now there, but always towards the corner. It sang a low song, scratched on the parchment.

Elaine put out her hand to guide it, to stop it from falling off the edge.

'No!' said the woman, sharply. 'Wait!'

The coin moved, directly now, as though it had been searching but had found its way. It slowed down, then shuddered to a halt – at the door of the great house, under the malign gaze of the monster.

'What does it mean?' asked Elaine, knowing the answer already.

'You will go where the coin rests.'

'I will leave there immediately and go into the city,' said Elaine. She looked at the eerie dark house.

'You must go to the house,' said the gypsy.

'At first,' said Elaine. 'But I will not go inside it.'

'No,' said the gypsy. 'You must go inside the house. You have chosen.'

'I will choose again,' said Elaine. She grabbed the coin, spun it again. The woman said nothing.

Again the coin hummed and sang. This time it made straight for the great house.

Elaine spun again. The coin made no sound this time, but sped impatiently to the house.

'The table is tilted,' said Elaine.

Silently, the gypsy took the coin and spun it. It hesitated, hummed, moved uncertainly, rolled in many directions, but never to the house, then it fell from the table and thudded onto the carpet. 'My future is not in this map,' said the gypsy.

'Nor mine,' said Elaine.

'You chose it. You made it.'

'I choose to ignore it,' said Elaine.

'But it will not ignore you,' said the gypsy.

Elaine stood up. 'Thank you,' she said, coldly. 'I will go now.'

'Before you know the place?'

'It is nothing to do with me,' said Elaine.

'Then, at least know where you will not go,' said the woman.

'How?'

'All the maps have names.'

'Show me.'

The woman turned the map over. Elaine read the words on its reverse. 'The Manor and Estates of Thorncliffe. No!'

'Yes,' said the gypsy. 'You will marry the Heir of Thorncliffe.'

'No. I won't! No!' Elaine fell back to her seat. The door swung open and a man came in.

'Get rid of her,' said Cam. 'Get rid of them both. They are trouble for us.'

The woman held up a hand to silence him.

Elaine's senses were racing. The incense, the colours, the warm closeness of Prophecy Tent, the touch of the woman, the mysterious look in her half-hidden eyes, and now the powerful intrusion of this young stranger: all these excited her more than she could understand.

'I am ready to go,' she said. But she knew she was not telling the truth. She had found a peace here that she had thought had disappeared for ever when the lawyers had signed their documents. Only a few hours had passed, and yet her whole world was changed.

'Go, then!' Cam snapped.

'Not until I have seen you.' Elaine spoke to the woman, but she could not keep her eyes from him.

'No,' said Cam.

'I promised,' said the woman. She lifted her hand to the veil. Elaine prepared herself for the age and ugliness it hid. 'But there is one thing, first.'

'Yes?'

'You refuse to marry the Heir of Thorncliffe?'

Elaine nodded.

Cam gasped.

Elaine looked at him. 'Why does he do that?' she asked.

Cam looked away.

'Why?' Elaine repeated.

'The Thorncliffes are not our friends,' said the woman.

'You too?'

'They refuse us their land,' said Cam.

'Once, many years ago,' said the woman, 'the Heir of Thorncliffe died, by poison.'

'Yes,' said Elaine.

'It was our people who made the potion,' said the woman. 'We have not been welcome since.'

Elaine looked at Cam. There was something else. 'Is that the only reason?' she asked.

'If you will really refuse him, there may be only one way out,' said the woman.

Elaine waited.

The woman took a small phial of green liquid from her robe.

'No!' said Cam.

'Be silent.' At the same time, she handed the phial to Elaine and drew the veil from her face.

Elaine was so surprised at the sight that met her eyes that she hardly noticed herself take the phial and put it in her own robe. The woman was young, almost as young as Elaine. And, most surprising of all, she was beautiful. Elaine turned her head slightly and saw Cam. She saw how he looked at the gypsy women, the love in his face, and she felt a pain like a knife in her chest.

CHAPTER VII

THE JOURNEY TO Thorncliffe was long and hard. Elaine felt bruised all over. Her head throbbed with a mixture of tiredness and fear and hatred.

Gwen sat opposite her, hands folded on her lap, eyes down when she did not doze. The jolting of the carriage was too much to allow her to sew the pane of embroidery that rested on her knees.

Elaine never let her eyes close for more than a moment. She strained to see everything, though the window was covered and she could not see out. It was as though her eyes burned through the blind and she saw everything as they passed it. And the intensity and concentration of her stare made her remember every twist and turn, every ditch and dip, every hill and hole. Elaine wanted to remember the road exactly, so that when she escaped – and she had no doubt that she would escape – then she would not be lost.

Gwen had tried, at first, to talk to her, but Elaine brushed her attempts aside with a contemptuous, 'Be silent, girl.'

Gwen wanted to hate her Mistress for this, but she could not. They had been too much together, too much to each other for this. She understood the anger that burned inside Elaine. And, although she wished she could make her understand, she knew it was not possible – not yet.

When they had returned from the gypsy camp, Elaine's father had been waiting for them, almost blind with rage, nearly speechless with anger. He had demanded to know where they had been. Elaine had refused to answer him, too proud to lie, too frightened to tell. He had demanded an answer from Gwen. Elaine's look ordered her to keep silent, but he was her Master and she could not refuse him as his daughter could, and, like Elaine, she would not lie.

And so, with no ceremony, no preparations, no farewells, they had been driven off into the night, to Thorncliffe.

Thorncliffe! With the squatting toads and the slimy walls. The home of thorns.

Even Gwen was frightened at the thought. Elaine hid her fear beneath anger, but the fear remained.

They travelled all through that night and the next day, resting only when darkness fell again. The horses were covered in sweat and white-lipped with fatigue. The inn was small and dark. Elaine and Gwen were hurried to a room and food was brought in to them.

'I'll kill him,' said Elaine. 'If he comes into this room I will kill him with my own hands.'

But neither Peter nor his father tried to come near her.

Elaine stayed awake all night, ready to fight him if he tried to enter, to talk to her, to reason with her, persuade her that it was for the best. He did not come.

Fresh horses pulled the carriage the next day, and then they stopped at another inn. That night Elaine tried to stay awake again, but she tumbled forward in the chair, waking Gwen. The girl tried to get her Mistress into bed, but when she touched her, Elaine's skin was burning and she was mumbling.

The fever raged all night.

Gwen wanted to stay at the inn until it had passed, but they carried Elaine to the carriage, wrapped her in blankets and let her burn her way to Thorncliffe.

'Nearly there,' the Lord of Thorncliffe promised. 'Soon after noon.'

'She can't travel like this,' said Gwen.

'She must.'

So Gwen sat and watched Elaine burn.

In her fever, Elaine felt every bump and hollow, yet she did not know where she was or what was happening to her. She dreamt, a hot feverish dream. The back of her throat was tight and burning.

Elaine lay in a wedding gown, her hands together on her breast. Her hair was brushed and curled, with flowers wound through it, and an ivory ribbon. She was dressed and prepared for marriage, but she lay near death.

Lying quite still, she was carried along, to her funeral, in a gypsy caravan. The warm hangings, the deep coloured carpet, the incense, the small brass burner, the scent of perfume all told her that she was being carried to the grave in the Tent of Prophecy.

She was the Bride of the Heir of Thorncliffe and she had taken poison. Not because she was being forced to marry him, but because he had been taken from her and she was being forced to marry another.

In her fever, she remembered that she had not asked her mother the name of that first Bride, the young girl who had loved Mikal. Now she knew. Her name was Elaine. And the Elaine who hated Peter and the Elaine who loved Mikal became one in the fevered dream.

But she was trapped inside this dead body, feeling every lurch of the caravan, hearing the snorting of the horses, the shouts of the gypsies. She was not dead, but sleeping. And through the deep sleep she could hear Mikal calling to her. She could feel his hands brushing her cheeks and her forehead, at one point she could feel his lips just touching hers.

If only her eyes weren't so heavy. If only she could open them and see his face, see him once more before the sleep deepened for ever and she died. Just to see him once more.

Elaine made a great effort; she forced herself to use her all her strength.

With one last effort she opened her eyes and looked straight at him. Mikal was there in the caravan, holding her, whispering to her, gently kissing her. 'You will be all right, Elaine. All right. Just hold on. You will be all right.'

And it was his face. The face of Cam. His strong arms held her. His lean, dark face looked down at her. His soft lips touched hers. His voice – gentle now, not mocking or bitter – comforted her. She responded to his kiss.

Elaine smiled and then lost consciousness. For ever?

Gwen clutched Elaine to her, trying to comfort her through the jolting of the carriage, praying that Thorncliffe would soon appear and that Elaine could rest and bathe her face in cool water to ease her fever. 'You will be all right, Elaine. All right. Just hold on. You will be all right,' she said.

Elaine opened her eyes and smiled back at her, but the gaze was far away, and Gwen knew that Elaine could not see her through the fever.

'All right down there?' There was a rap on the door. The Lord of Thorncliffe, riding alongside, shouted in, 'Soon be there.'

Gwen lifted the corner of the blind. And there, on the brow of the hill, stood the Manor of Thorncliffe, the nightmare house of their childhood. At last, she saw it.

CHAPTER VIII

'YOU WILL BE all right, Elaine. All right.
Just hold on. You will be all right.'
Elaine felt herself coming up and up,
through warm river water, and into the air. She
gasped, and felt, for the first time, as though
she could breathe freely.

She opened her eyes and looked around. It
was no river-bank, but a large, light bed chamber. The sunlight filtered through a gauze at the
window, embroidered with honeysuckle and cle-
matis and tiny birds, darting through the leaves.
It splashed against the walls and dappled them
with warm patterns. A bowl of rose petals lay
at the side of her bed. Red and pink and gold
and white, and fragrant with the scent of
summer. The fine counterpane was set with
fragile threads of gold and silver. The pillows
were soft and full and cool against her cheek.
Her hair, undone and loose, spread around her
face.

'Elaine?' said Gwen.

'Of course it is.'

Gwen hugged her.

'Why do you ask, silly?' said Elaine.

'This is not the first time you have looked at
me in the last week,' said Gwen. 'But you have

never known me before, never answered when I have spoken your name.'

'Week?'

'At least,' said Gwen. 'You have been very ill.'

'Nonsense,' said Elaine. 'Look.' She tried to move her legs, to step out of the bed, but they would only move slowly, painfully.

'See.'

Elaine lay back. 'A week?'

'We thought you were going to die,' said Gwen. 'You were so hot. And so restless.'

'The fever drives you hard,' said another voice, one that Elaine knew but could not place. She looked around the room.

The woman had been hidden by the heavy drapes at the side of the bed. Elaine saw her and recognized the lovely face and young eyes of the gypsy fortune-teller.

'What are you doing here?' she demanded.

'Elaine,' said Gwen, 'Rebekka saved your life.'

'Not quite.' The gypsy smiled.

'Yes,' Gwen insisted. 'You did. You know you did.'

Elaine was at last beginning to understand. 'Where did you bring me?' she asked. She took in the room with its lovely walls and curtains, its delicate shades and colours, the light, airy atmosphere. 'At least you rescued me from Thorncliffe.'

'Not at all,' said the gypsy woman. 'This is Thorncliffe Manor.'

*

53

It was nearly another week before Elaine was strong enough to leave her room and walk in the gardens of the Manor. In all that time the thing she had feared most had so far not happened. Peter had not appeared, and nor had the Lord of Thorncliffe.

'I won't marry him,' Elaine insisted, at least ten times every day. 'I will *never* marry the Heir of Thorncliffe.'

Gwen would not argue at first, but Elaine made her.

'You know I won't marry him, don't you?' she insisted, demanding an answer.

'I would,' said Gwen. 'If I had to. He could be worse.'

'You said that before,' said Elaine. 'I won't. *Ever!*'

'You have nowhere else to go,' Gwen said.

'I'll go with the gypsies,' said Elaine. 'They will steal me away.'

'With Rebekka?' asked Gwen.

Elaine hesitated. 'Yes,' she said. But it was not Rebekka's face that came to her mind every time she planned to escape with the caravans.

Even though the fever had left her, Elaine still slept fitfully and she dreamt every night. Vivid, powerful dreams that made her cry out a name, that caused her heart to beat wildly, and sometimes set her sitting up in bed, hot and frantic, so that she woke again in the morning feeling more tired than when she had laid her face on the pillow.

She lay in bed and saw Mikal's face over hers. Yet it was the face of Cam, and the strong body and the dark hair in the silver clip. And she longed to let him pick her up and carry her away, out of Thorncliffe, to safety and to freedom. To the city in the map with the towers and spires and winding streets and narrow alleys.

But she always woke before he could lift her. And she sobbed with anger and loneliness.

Gwen, who heard Elaine crying out in the night, kept her silence when Elaine agreed that it was Rebekka who would take her away. 'And he hasn't been near me,' said Elaine. 'Not since the day we arrived. I haven't seen the Heir of Thorncliffe. Perhaps he'll never come back. Perhaps he'll leave me alone for ever.'

But she put her hand into her robe and felt for the phial of poison as she said it, determined never to marry Peter Thorncliffe.

'Perhaps,' agreed Gwen. But she did not believe it either.

Gwen was not surprised when the day arrived when Peter Thorncliffe again stated his demand that Elaine should be his wife and stay there for ever.

He did not come in person.

'He is too much of a coward,' said Elaine.

Gwen held the box that Peter's servant had delivered, along with the message: 'The Heir will be here soon. You are to wear this to welcome him.'

The bracelet of thorns lay, beautiful, against the velvet.

'It is lovely,' said Gwen.

Elaine glanced at it.

'See. It catches the light. Look how it winds and twists.'

'Like the lying mouth of a Thorncliffe,' said Elaine.

Yet something about the bracelet attracted her, drew her to it. She looked properly this time.

'It would cut you,' she said at last. 'The thorns are too sharp. And they go the wrong way.'

Gwen picked it up. 'There are two strands,' she said. 'They intertwine. It would be safe enough.'

'You try it,' said Elaine.

'I couldn't. It wouldn't be right.'

'I don't mind.'

Elaine felt her chest grow tight as she said the words. She hated the sight of the thing, yet she was drawn to it. She would not wear it herself; yet she wanted to see it worn. She could not touch it; yet she resented Gwen for touching it.

'I can't,' said Gwen.

'Oh, do it!'

Gwen took up the bracelet carefully. She tried to slide her hand inside. A thorn prevented her. It scratched Gwen and drew a red line on her hand.

'Go on,' said Elaine. She was holding her

breath, longing to see the hand go in, frightened of the pain and the blood. 'Push.'

Gwen hesitated.

'Turn it round,' said Elaine. 'Make it fit.'

Gwen twisted her hand and tried to get the thorns out of the way. 'Ouch!'

Elaine bit her lip. 'Go on,' she urged again.

'I can't.' Gwen was bleeding freely now, and the blood stained the brightness of the silver. 'You try it,' she said to Elaine. 'I hate the thing.'

She threw the bracelet on to the counterpane and the thorns pricked blood into the pale damask.

Elaine took it gently. She turned it over and over in her hands, looking for a way through the thorns. 'If we could twist the two strands,' she said, 'I think it would be all right.'

'Never,' said Gwen. 'It's a trap.'

Elaine dropped the bracelet back into the box, where it sank into the folds of velvet. 'Yes,' she agreed. 'Like Thorncliffe. It's a trap. And we won't fall into it. We'll escape.'

'They say,' said Rebekka, who was standing behind them, 'that only the Heir of Thorncliffe can make the Jewel safe for his bride.'

'Rebekka,' said Elaine, 'I must escape.'

'The thorns will keep you here, said Rebekka. 'There is no escape.'

Elaine put her hand inside her robe and clutched the phial of poison. 'There is one way,' she said to Rebekka. 'Can you help me to find another?'

'I do not think so,' said Rebekka. 'You are the Bride of the Heir of Thorncliffe. It was always in your future.'

'No,' said Elaine. 'I chose that map. I can choose another.'

'It chose you,' said Rebekka. 'You will marry the Heir of Thorncliffe.'

'No.'

A sudden clatter of hoofs on the cobbled courtyard made Gwen run to the window.

'He's here,' she said.

CHAPTER IX

THERE WAS NO time for Rebekka to disappear before the knock on Elaine's door announced Peter Thorncliffe's arrival, so she slipped on to the bed and drew the curtains round her.

Peter did not wait for Elaine to answer, but stepped straight into the room.

'Please wait!' Elaine snapped.

'There is no time,' said Peter.

'You will wait outside until I call,' said Elaine. She turned her back to him, looked out of the window and waited for him to leave.

'Very well.' The anger was etched on his face, but he left.

Gwen touched Elaine's shoulder and she could feel the strong, rapid beat of her heart. 'Don't be afraid, Elaine.'

'Afraid! I'm not afraid!' Elaine's voice was low, so that Peter should not hear, but it was breathless and jerky with passion. 'I am furious that he should just walk in like that. Who does he think he is?'

Gwen knew the answer was, 'The Heir of Thorncliffe. Your husband, soon.' But she also knew that she must not say the words.

'I won't see him,' said Elaine.

'You will have to see him,' said Gwen.

The window was high and the wall fell steeply to a rocky incline below. There was no other way out and they both knew it.

Elaine touched the clip which held her hair tight to her head. She felt as though she was being gripped by something malignant and grasping.

'I will meet him now,' she said. 'Show him in.'

Gwen opened the door. Peter was waiting outside. She nodded to him, and he walked past her, into the room. 'The wedding is arranged for three days' time,' he said.

'Never,' said Elaine.

Peter looked her straight in the eyes. 'I have come to hate the idea as much as you,' he said. 'But you will wear the Thorncliffe Jewel, please.'

'You want me to tear myself to pieces? Is that how you care for me?'

'I don't understand.' Peter's face showed genuine puzzlement.

'Show him, Gwen.'

She showed Peter the scratches and the blood, the deep tear in her hand.

'Of course,' said Peter. 'Only the Bride of Thorncliffe, only the Daughter of the Wolds can wear the bracelet without harm. It is our tradition.'

Elaine remembered Rebekka's words. 'That's not right,' she said. 'Only the Heir of Thorncliffe can put the bracelet on.'

Peter frowned. 'Where did you hear this?'

'It is our tradition,' Elaine said.

'Then I will do it,' said Peter. He took the bracelet, and unwillingly, but out of fascinated interest, Elaine allowed him to try to put it on her wrist. At the first sign of resistance and a scratch, he stopped. 'I can't do it.'

'Then I can't wear it,' said Elaine.

They glared at each other in hatred.

'We should stop now,' said Elaine. And she allowed the anger in her voice to die down, allowed him to come closer to her fear. 'You said that you would rather never see me again.'

'Yes,' said Peter, 'that is true. But,' he continued, 'three days from now, you will be my wife. And though I hate the prospect as much as you, I will do it from duty. Be ready.'

And he slammed the door.

The echoes of the anger died down. Gwen and Elaine kept their eyes from one another – and neither of them spoke. Peter's angry steps died away in the distance, but his presence seemed to remain with them.

Rebekka drew aside the curtain and climbed down from the bed.

'You were wrong,' said Elaine.

'If you say so.'

'He didn't know how to put the bracelet on.'

'No?'

'I'm leaving tonight,' said Elaine. 'Will you help me?'

She opened the door. Two men stood outside.

61

'Sorry, miss,' said one, 'you must stay in your room.'

'Step aside.'

The man did not need to push Elaine back. He was too large for her to thrust aside, and she did feel as though she could reach out her hand to touch him. She closed the door.

'We're prisoners, until the wedding,' said Gwen.

'There will be no wedding,' said Elaine, fiercely. '*Never.*'

'Three days from today,' Rebekka said, 'you will marry the Heir of Thorncliffe. You will marry him. It is your future.'

Elaine took the phial of poison from her robe.

Rebekka's face was excited, ecstatic. 'The past always comes round again,' she said. Her eyes had the distant look they had taken on in the Tent of Prophecy.

'No!' said Gwen.

Rebekka took the phial from Elaine and opened it.

CHAPTER X

ELAINE WAS DRESSED for bed, in a simple white gown, tied at the neck. Or for the grave, Gwen thought. It would make a good shroud.

'There is no other way,' Rebekka said. 'We must let her go with her destiny. She is the Daughter of the Wolds.'

'Yes,' said Elaine, 'there is no other way.' She lay on the bed and waited for Rebekka.

'Even you,' said Rebekka. 'You must follow your destiny.'

Gwen laughed bitterly. 'Oh, yes,' she said. 'Orphan before I was born. Servant all my life. I know my destiny. I always have. So why should Elaine escape hers by dying? That's a coward's way out. Let her accept it as I always have.'

'You accept your destiny?' asked Rebekka.

'Of course.'

'Would you accept it so readily if you knew what it was?'

'Yes!'

'Very well.' Rebekka opened her bag and took out a pack of cards and a smaller bag. She held the cards out to Gwen. 'Will you take one?'

Gwen shook her head.

Elaine sat up on the bed. Her eyes were shining and she was breathing quickly. 'Go on,' she said, 'go on!'

Gwen took a card from near the bottom of the pile. She began to turn it over.

'Not yet,' said Rebekka. 'Take something from the bag.'

Gwen put her hand into the bag, felt around. 'Shall I choose?' she asked. 'Or shall I take the first thing I get?'

'It makes no difference,' said Rebekka, 'whether you choose your destiny or let it choose you. It will come to the same.'

Gwen drew out a hank of damask cloth.

'Now,' said Rebekka. 'The card first.'

Gwen turned it over. It was a queen.

'Not a servant's card,' said Rebekka.

Gwen grimaced. 'Once a servant, always a servant.'

Rebekka tipped out the contents of the bag. 'You could have chosen an acorn. Or a comb, or a ruby – a real one – or a silver star, or twenty other things. Yes?'

'Yes,' agreed Gwen.

Rebekka put the cloth under Gwen's eyes. 'See the fine embroidery?'

'Yes.'

'What is it?'

Elaine slipped off the bed and ran across. 'It's briars,' she said. 'All tangled together.'

'Thorns,' said Rebekka. 'Gwen's destiny is to be Mistress of Thorncliffe.'

There was a long silence.

'So I must die, then?' said Elaine.

They talked long into the night, in quiet voices that would not penetrate the door.

'I don't believe it,' said Gwen, over and over. 'I don't believe it. I can't believe it.'

'It's true,' said Elaine. 'I promised I would never tell you. And I feel disloyal now. But I have to. I was only told last year. The papers were all signed, but I wasn't shown them.'

'So it might not be true,' said Gwen.

'You know it is. If I die without children you will be the Daughter of the Wolds. They love you. They always have. You have always been my sister.'

'Why was I not told?'

'Because they thought it would not be fair to you, to let you think that one day you might be Mistress of the Wolds, and then for it not to happen. But the arrangements had to made made. Just in case I never married or I died young.'

'But if you did marry, I was to be just a servant?'

Elaine hugged Gwen. 'You know that isn't true,' she said. 'If I married, you would come with me, as my sister, not my servant. Here you are.'

Gwen did not answer.

Elaine said what they had not dared to say. 'And you wanted to marry Peter.'

'No. I did not want to.'

'You said you would.'

'It was a joke.'

And they knew it was no joke.

'I did not think,' said Elaine. 'I was so angry with myself, I did not think it through. If I die, you will be the Daughter of the Wolds, so you will be the Mistress of Thorncliffe. He will have to marry you. The contract says so.'

'And it is your destiny,' said Rebekka. 'You chose it.'

'I don't want it,' said Gwen. 'I won't ever do it. Ever.'

'Listen,' said Elaine, 'this is what we must do.'

The look of hatred in Gwen's eyes burned into Rebekka, but the gypsy woman seemed to try to ignore it. She mopped Elaine's brow, wet from the fever again. Elaine moaned.

'How long has she been like this?' Peter asked.

'Since just after you said she must marry you in three days,' said Gwen. 'We sent the guards away, and then this gypsy woman arrived.'

Rebekka was glad that Peter accepted the explanation.

'Can you help her?' he asked.

Gwen saw the real compassion in his eyes, and her heart went out to him. He was trapped in this as much as Elaine was.

'I will do all I can to save her,' said Rebekka.

'If it is anything to do with me,' said Peter, 'I will release her from the contract.' He picked up an empty phial. 'What is this?'

Gwen looked away. Rebekka took it from him. 'A healing potion,' she said.

Peter waited for more but when no further explanation came, he walked out.

All through the night Elaine raved and tossed with the fever. Peter came every hour to see how she was, and frowned more deeply each time as the fever seemed to draw her ever deeper into oblivion.

'Do everything,' he said to Rebekka. 'Do you understand?'

'Of course.'

Just before dawn, Elaine screamed out. Peter ran in. Elaine's body was jerking and thrashing about on the bed. He grabbed her shoulders and tried to calm her. Gwen flew at him and dragged him away.

'Leave her alone! Haven't you done enough?'

'I have done nothing. I release her from all contracts. Just make her better.'

Rebekka dabbed at Elaine's temples. Elaine relaxed, sank back into the mattress, moaned again, then went rigid.

Peter sprang to the bedside. 'What's happening?'

Elaine sighed, breathed out gently, and then seemed to sink right into the bed.

Rebekka held a looking glass to Elaine's lips. No mist clouded it.

She drew the sheet over Elaine's face.

'She is free of any contract now.'

CHAPTER XI

THE FUNERAL PROCESSION was slow and silent, save for the beat of a single, muffled drum.

Elaine's body, clothed in the white gown, lay on a flower-decked bier. Lilies and white damask roses twined round and round her body and threaded through her hair. The thorns made Gwen want to cry again. The morning sun just capped the tops of the elms; the mist still swirled round their ankles as the bearers carried the white body across the grass to the small chapel by the river.

Gwen's feet were wet with dew and she shivered.

Peter walked immediately behind the bier, his head straight, his eyes level. Then he suddenly stumbled. Instinctively, and without time to stop herself, Gwen reached out a swift hand to steady him. He gripped her arm and found his balance. Gwen tried to take her arm from him, but he held it for just a moment longer than he needed to. They looked at each other for a moment, each needing someone to help them through this terrible dawn. Then they fell into step again, their eyes directly ahead.

There was no door to the chapel, no windows.

It was open to the air, not derelict, yet a ruin of what it had been in former years. The stones were crumbling back into the earth. Yet it was light and clean and there was no moss, no mould in it. Elaine's body was gently lowered to the broad flagstone floor.

Peter sent the bearers out of the chapel, to stand guard at the door. Then he took the box with the Jewel of Thorncliffe in it and laid it next to Elaine.

'You should keep it,' said Gwen. 'It was never hers.'

Peter thought. Then he said, 'She is the last Daughter of the Wolds. She should have it.'

'It belongs to the Mistress of Thorncliffe,' said Rebekka. 'It is not yours to give.'

'It belongs to the past,' said Peter. 'Let it die with her.'

A scuffling noise from outside caught Gwen's attention. 'Elaine will not be safe here,' she said. 'There are animals – rats, foxes.'

'The men will stand guard until she is buried,' said Peter. 'They will keep danger away. And it is only for one day and one night. Tomorrow she will be laid to rest for ever.'

The scuffling repeated itself. Gwen looked through the empty lancet, but she could not see anything.

'I'll stay, too,' she said.

'If you wish,' said Peter.

Gwen leant against a stone pillar and watched.

Peter kept upright. Rebekka sank to the floor and sat with her back against the cold stone.

The sun rose in the sky. The mist melted away. The birds began to fill the air with song. The shadows hardened from blurred edges to straight lines and then began to lengthen across the flagged floor.

As the chapel grew warm and light, Gwen found herself slowly sobbing, in painful, silent spasms. Tears ran down her face and she was too tired, too wretched to brush them away.

Peter felt, rather than heard, her grief. He looked at her and flinched. 'Come on,' he said. He took her arm, and lifted her to her feet. This time, Gwen did not resist him. 'You must eat.'

'I cannot eat,' Gwen protested. But she allowed herself to be led away, leaving Rebekka alone in the chapel with Elaine.

As he left, Peter spoke to the guards. 'If she needs anything, obey her.'

For a long time Rebekka sat, still as ever, listening to the gentle breeze in the branches over her head, the rustling of small, harmless creatures, and the same eager scuffling that Gwen had heard earlier. Then she stood up and went to the guards. 'You can go now,' she said. 'I will wait another hour. Then you can return.'

They protested, but Rebekka had heard Peter. 'You have your orders. I need something,' she said. 'I need you to go away for an hour.'

When they had gone, Rebekka knelt by Elaine's side and put her hand on the brow. 'Soon,' she whispered, 'soon you will be free for ever.'

The scuffling noise grew loud, and a figure, dark and swift, slipped through the lancet and dropped lightly to the ground.

Rebekka looked up.

The tall figure of Cam towered over her. 'You've killed her! Because you were jealous of her. You could have saved her life.'

'No,' said Rebekka. 'Listen.'

'I would never have stayed with you,' said Cam. 'You know that.'

'I know. I did not want you to.'

'Liar!'

'No.'

'Yes! You are a liar. You would have used me up and thrown me away. And I would have let you. I loved you. But not when I had seen her.'

'No, Cam,' said Rebekka. 'Listen to me. It is time you understood. You are old enough now to be told.'

'I know already. I know all about you. You're a witch. Just a gypsy witch. Well, she's not staying here. I couldn't have her alive, but I'll have her now she's dead.'

'No! You can't!'

'Can't you see?' said Cam. 'I hate you. You'll go on and on and on, for ever, in the way ̲̅ches do. I'll take Elaine and I'll bury her ̲̅only I know. She'll be mine in death.'

̲̅ped down and lifted her over his ̲̅single movement.

Rebekka grabbed the box with the Jewel of Thorncliffe. 'Listen,' she said, urgently. 'You've got to listen.'

Cam pushed her aside and was gone.

Gwen sank into a chair and breathed deeply. Her face was relaxing from the effort of grief. Her breathing was slowing down. Peter sent for water.

'It's all right,' he said. 'It will be all right.'

'She gone,' said Gwen. 'She's gone for ever. She was my friend.'

'She was your sister,' Peter said.

Gwen sipped the water, spilling a little with the unsteadiness of her hand. Peter waited for her to speak again, not liking to rush her.

'And now I must go, too,' said Gwen.

'Where?'

Gwen looked into the glass, keeping her eyes away from him.

'I will arrange for your safe return to the Wolds,' said Peter.

'I cannot return,' said Gwen. 'I have let them lose their daughter.'

Peter hesitated before he said, 'You could stay here. There will always be a place for you at Thorncliffe. If you would like it.'

'No,' said Gwen, though she seemed reluctant to say it. 'I cannot stay here, and I cannot return to the Wolds. Not after what I have done.'

'It was not your fault,' said Peter.

'Don't you understand?' said Gwen. 'Do you really not know?'

Peter sprang to his feet. 'What?'

'The fever was cured. It did not come back of itself. It was the gypsy woman who made her ill again.'

'No!'

'Yes. You picked up the phial that had the potion in it. I thought you would know.'

'You are lying!' Peter shouted.

'No,' said Gwen. 'I wish I could lie about it. I have sent Elaine away from here for ever.'

Peter smashed the glass of water.

'I will kill that meddling gypsy!' he gasped. And he ran out into the sunlight and towards the chapel.

CHAPTER XII

THE PHIAL WAS cool and smooth in Elaine's hand. She looked anxiously at Rebekka. 'It will be all right, won't it?'

Rebekka nodded. 'It's the only way to escape. You're locked in here. You'll be married in two days' time.'

Gwen bit her lip but kept her silence. She had tried to argue with Elaine, but the young woman in the white gown had become her Mistress again, not her friend or her sister. Gwen could not contain herself any more. 'Don't do it. Please. I can't bear to lose you. I don't want to live without you.'

Elaine smiled. 'Dear Gwen, you'll be all right. You'll be Mistress of Thorncliffe.'

'I'll . . .' began Gwen. But she stopped when Elaine raised the phial to her lips and drank it down in a single gulp.

'No!' shouted Gwen.

Elaine fell back into the pillow. Rebekka took the phial from her lips.

By the time Gwen reached her, Elaine's brow had already begun to burn with the fever.

Elaine could still hear them through the fever. She lay in the hot bed and heard Peter demand to know what was going on; then, other voices and an argument. Sometimes the words were clear; at other times they became like the hum of insects, or the murmuring of trees in the night.

Then there was the water again. Elaine loved this best of all. The freedom – to swim without the restricting clothes she had to wear, her hair free and floating behind her, the sense of being lifted up by the water and carried along, as though head high in a procession.

Once, she thought that Cam was swimming with her. That his hair too was free of its silver clip and that he bore her in his arms through the warm water. She turned her head to him and tried to murmur his name, but the water filled her mouth, so she slipped back into the delicious floating.

And then she rested on a river bank, and Cam took her in his arms and she turned her head to his face and knew that she could not have married Peter once she had seen this gypsy with the black hair and the strong white face and the lithe, quick step that let him dart into the trees and in and out of her life.

And then there was silence and darkness and nothing.

The sun was high and hot as Cam left the chapel. He ran as swiftly as Rebekka, almost too quickly for her to keep up. He headed straight for the cover of the woods, to be out of sight of pursuers, in the direction of the gypsy encampment.

As soon as he saw them, the hunched man kicked dirt into the fire, pushed his fingers in his mouth, and gave a loud, shrill whistle.

As if by magic, the clothes were snatched from trees, pots were emptied and thrown into caravans, ponies were harnessed, wheels began to trundle along.

'Twelve days,' said the hunched man. 'Barton's Ford.'

The instruction went round the group, and the caravans set off in all directions, no longer a band of gypsies, but single vans or pairs, going their own ways.

Cam bore Elaine to the Tent of Prophecy. The roses and lilies in her hair were tangled and torn. Her skin was still pale as the rose, as wan as the lilies. Cam gently lowered her to the bed. He gasped for breath after the exertion of carrying her so far and so fast. His eyes were fighting the dimness of the caravan. The fragrance of the incense made him light headed. For a long time he looked down at Elaine, then he put his lips on her cheek and let them rest there.

'We have no time,' said Rebekka. 'They'll be following us. Drive on. I'll look after Elaine.'

'No. I don't want you around,' said Cam. 'Go.'

'Don't be stupid. She can't stay here alone. She'll fall to the floor when you hit the first rut in the path. Drive. And quickly. They'll be confused when they see we've separated, but they'll follow every trail sooner or later. We've got to get away as soon as we can.'

Cam grimaced, but he knew she was right. 'You killed her,' he said. 'I never want to see you again.'

'Drive,' she said.

Cam left the caravan and scrambled up to the high seat. He flicked the reins and they were off.

Rebekka drew Elaine's hair back from her brow and arranged it neatly. She wove the flowers through her hair.

Cam called down, 'I never belonged with you. I'm leaving for ever.'

Rebekka sprinkled some cool, scented water on Elaine's forehead.

'I thought I could stay. I thought I could make it work. With you.' Cam laughed. 'That's a joke, isn't it? Eh? The outsider, the foundling boy, marrying the gypsy queen.'

'Not the queen,' said Rebekka. 'And you were not a foundling.'

'No,' he agreed. 'Not the queen. Better than the queen. The gypsy of gypsies. The wise woman. The old one. Eh? That's right, isn't it? How old are you? How many husbands have you had?'

Rebekka smiled and anointed Elaine's lips with a sweet salve. 'I am as old as the Tent of Prophecy,' she said. 'I came here, time immemorial. I have had many husbands, but I have never married.'

'Riddle!' said Cam. 'Gypsy riddles. When will you tell the truth?'

'You were not always so contemptuous of gypsies,' said Rebekka, 'when you wanted to be one of us.'

'You said I never could. You didn't want me. Well, now you can't have me. I'm taking Elaine, and I'm going to bury her.'

'You will not bury her,' said Rebekka.

'I will. I couldn't have her alive, but I won't let her leave me in death.'

'It is not her destiny,' said Rebekka. 'You will not bury her.'

Cam urged the ponies on harder. 'I've done with your gypsy nonsense. I don't believe in your destiny. That's just for gypsies. I don't belong with you. I never did. I'm a foundling. Remember?'

'No,' said Rebekka. 'That isn't right.'

The wagon came to a sudden stop. Cam put his head through the small window and stared at her. 'What do you mean?'

'You are not a foundling?'

'You said so. You always said so.'

'No.'

'You said I was no gypsy. That my parents were dead. That I was left with you.'

'Yes.'

'And you lied?'

'No. It is true. But you were not a foundling. You were born in the gypsy camp. Your parents travelled with us, though neither was one of us. They were outsiders.'

'Wait,' said Cam. 'I don't understand.'

He let the reins fall slack, and was about to climb down when the caravan was jolted and jarred as though a bull had charged into it.

Cam shouted out in pain. Then another voice drowned his cries.

'Got you! Gypsy dog!'

CHAPTER XIII

THE SUDDEN ATTACK gave Peter the advantage and he took it. But Cam had all the experience of a gypsy life, all the skill and training of one who travelled and lived on his wits. Years of pitching and striking camp, of riding rough ground and travelling long days and nights had given his body a hard, keen edge that Peter could not match.

As soon as his head stopped swimming from the surprise, Cam took in the danger he was in and reacted. He let his body go limp and dead. Peter was fooled by the show of defeat and he relaxed his grip. Cam immediately twisted under him, punched a fist into Peter's face and wriggled out of his grasp. He sprang to his feet, waited for Peter to recover and then leapt on him again with another blow to the side of the head.

Peter staggered to the ground.

'No,' said Rebekka, and she stepped between them.

'Mind out,' Peter gasped. 'I'll fight my own battles.'

'You would lose,' she said.

'Get out of the way,' Peter said, but he made no attempt to rise. He breathed deeply, gathering his thoughts as he waited. He had chosen the right path. Elaine was in the wagon. He knew she was. And this gypsy boy, man. What was he doing? Peter's mind raced. Time. That was what he wanted, needed, more than anything. He knew he could not overpower them both. So, what to do?

'Yes,' Cam said. 'Get out of the way. Let us finish it off. He killed Elaine. Now, let me kill him.'

Peter climbed to his feet. 'You lying gypsy,' he said. 'I never killed her. She might have lived if it had not been for this witch and her potions.'

'He is no gypsy, any more than you are,' said Rebekka softly. 'And you are wrong. She did not die of a fever.'

The two young men stood, side by side, and stared at her.

Rebekka's face, young and lovely, seemed to grow old. Her eyes were tired and her smile was too wise for her lips.

'She drank the Thorncliffe Potion,' said Rebekka. 'I gave it to her. It was the only way to get her out of the wedding.'

'You killed her!' said Peter.

'I gave it to her, just as I did all those years ago, to the other Daughter of the Wolds.'

Peter sneered. 'You're mad.'

'Wait,' said Cam. 'Listen to her. Then you may take her away. But I warn you, she is dangerous. She will not let you kill her. She is as old as time itself.' He looked at Rebekka.

'Did you? Did you give the poison to the first Daughter of the Wolds?'

'I gave her the Thorncliffe Potion,' sad Rebekka. 'And I took her body away, as I have taken Elaine's. But this time, I think, the end will be different. Come. Let us see her before we go back to Thorncliffe.' She led them to the caravan. 'Be gentle,' she said. 'Be careful.'

Peter's heart raced as he stepped inside. The fragrant incense drugged his mind immediately. The warm hangings, the soft rugs, the flickering lamps made him feel out of control and helpless. This was another world, and it was as mysterious to him as the other side of the moon.

Cam went straight to Elaine and put his hand on her forehead.

Peter choked back a sob.

'You have done this thing, Cam,' said Rebekka softly. 'She came to this Tent once before. You could have carried her off then. But you did not welcome her.'

'I wanted to,' said Cam.

'But you told her to go away. You said we did not welcome strangers. Yet we welcomed your family when they were in need.' Then she looked at Peter. 'You have done this thing too,' she said. 'You made her go to Thorncliffe. You would have made her marry you.'

'I had no choice.'

'We always have a choice,' Rebekka said, picking up the box and giving it to Cam. 'She should wear this now. Put it on her.'

Cam opened the box and gave a cry of surprise. He picked up the bracelet with its two interlocking strands. 'It's twisted,' he said. Then he flicked it round and made the thorns point inwards, towards each other.

Safe now, the bracelet slid smoothly on to Elaine's wrist as Cam lifted her small, slender hand.

Peter stared at him.

'What is it?' Cam demanded angrily.

'You made the Thorncliffe Jewel safe,' said Peter. 'How did you know?'

The blackness cleared, and the silence dissolved into whispering.

Elaine felt herself rise up and up through the water until she burst into the air and could breathe freely.

Her eyes were heavy, too heavy to open. Fingertips brushed her forehead. Delicate hands dressed her hair and arranged it around her face. A soft caress stroked her lips with something cool and fragrant and soothing.

Birds, and the rustle of trees and the soft humming of a song. Then a sudden cry and a jolt, and then the fingers left her and Elaine drifted again.

Until her hand was lifted and she felt a circle of briars slip over her wrist and lie there.

All at once she was on a bed in a chamber in Thorncliffe, and the briars had grown up the walls and round the Manor and all over the parkland. And she was enfolded in their thorns and their roses. She felt the panic rising in her, felt the threat of the thorns.

She tried to cry out, but she could not.

Then, she saw the image of a man, standing against the sun, through the tangled briars. His hair was caught back, behind his head. His arms were raised and he prepared to strike. With controlled but deadly strength he dashed a blade against the thorns and parted the briars and forced his way through, plunging, ever more and more, stronger and fiercer, ever faster, again and again, until he had penetrated to the very heart of the tangled nest.

And when he reached her, she recognized him as the Heir of Thorncliffe. Saw his black hair, knew his strong face, loved his dark eyes. She reached out her hands and called him.

'Mikal!'

Cam had no time to answer Peter's question. His hand still held Elaine's wrist and the thorn bracelet was under his palm, when her lifeless body stirred.

Peter gasped. Rebekka bit her lip. Cam gripped Elaine's wrist as though he would never let her go.

Her chest rose and fell. Her breathing was sharp and rapid and eager.

'What's happening?' Peter demanded.

'Hush,' said Rebekka.

Elaine's eyelids flickered. Her lips parted and

she gasped and panted. Her eyes opened. For a second she stared round, lost and startled. Then she saw Cam. Her eyes fastened on him. She pulled his hand to her and gripped it tight and cried, 'Mikal!'

CHAPTER XIV

ELAINE AND GWEN hugged each other and cried, and hugged tighter than ever.

'I didn't believe it,' said Gwen, 'Not in my heart. I did in my head. I knew it would be all right in my head. But I couldn't accept it when I saw you in the fever and then so still and dead. And when I saw how terrible it was for Peter, I wanted to tell him, so much.' And she looked at Peter. He returned her look with even greater intensity.

'How could you not tell?' Gwen then asked Rebekka. 'How could you keep such a secret?'

'My life is secrets,' said Rebekka. 'And I have kept this one for hundreds of years.'

Peter rubbed his forehead and frowned. 'It isn't really true, is it? You aren't the woman who gave the first Daughter of the Wolds the Thorncliffe Potion.'

'I am the same,' said Rebekka. 'Can't you see?'

They looked at her and they could see in her eyes the age that was not on her cheeks.

'I gave her the Potion and she was carried off for dead.'

'I was her,' said Elaine. 'Somehow. When I was drugged. I know I was her. I thought Cam was Mikal.'

'Yes,' said Rebekka. 'I gave it to Mikal when he was sentenced to follow her. The effects are powerful but short-lived. The semblance of death is perfect, but the recovery is complete. They married and came with us, following the gypsies. And there has been a Thorncliffe with us ever since. Cam is the last of the line. His parents died in a flood three weeks after he was born. He is not a member of our people.'

Peter said, 'Well, he is welcome here.'

'That is not yours to say,' said Rebekka quietly.

In the silence that followed they understood what had not been clear to them before. All except Cam.

'What do you mean?' he asked.

Rebekka reached her hand out and unfastened the silver clip from his hair. She handed it to Elaine.

'Oh,' she said. 'Gwen. Look.'

It was a perfect replica of the Thorncliffe Jewel, about a quarter of the size.

'So you knew how to make the bracelet safe,' Elaine said.

Still Cam was puzzled.

'Tell me,' he said to Rebekka. 'What is happening?'

'You are the Heir of Thorncliffe,' she said. 'Or you were, when you were born. You have been the rightful Lord of Thorncliffe ever since you were three weeks old. Welcome to your Estates.'

'I don't want it,' said Cam.

'No?'

'Then what do you want?'

Cam and Elaine looked at each other.

'I don't want it either,' said Elaine. 'I never wanted to be Mistress of Thorncliffe.'

Gwen gave a nervous laugh. 'This makes a mockery of your fortune-telling,' she said.

'Does it?'

'Yes. All those destinies were wrong.'

Rebekka looked at the four faces. 'Will you take her?' she asked Cam.

'If she will have me,' he answered.

'With all my heart and soul,' said Elaine. 'But I will not stay here.'

'It is all the same to your destiny,' said Rebekka. 'As long as you marry the Heir of Thorncliffe you may go where you like.'

'Anywhere?'

'Yes.'

'There is a city,' said Elaine. 'I saw it once on a map. With winding lanes and spires and squares, and gardens in courtyards, with fountains and . . .'

'We will go tomorrow,' said Cam.

'But what about Thorncliffe?' asked Gwen.

Rebekka ignored her and turned to Peter. 'Will you take her?' she asked him.

Elaine's eyes flashed in angry challenge, but Peter did not look at her. He looked at Gwen. 'If she will join her life with mine,' he said. 'I will. If she will have a pauper with no home, and no money. But who can ask that?'

'I'll go anywhere with you,' said Gwen. 'We don't need this place.'

'But your destiny,' said Rebekka, 'is to be Mistress of Thorncliffe.'

'Stay here, Peter,' said Cam. 'Be Steward of Thorncliffe. Have it as your home. Run it as your Estate.' To Gwen he said, 'Be Mistress of Thorncliffe as his wife.'

'Where will you go?' asked Gwen.

'A city. A sea. Another shore. Who knows?'

The two young women hugged each other again.

'I will be back one day,' said Elaine, 'to see you.'

'Soon?'

'One day.'

Elaine looked back at the severe outline of Thorncliffe Manor. Peter stood, framed against the light, as he had done in her vision in the Tent of Prophecy. He raised his arm in farewell.

Elaine turned her back on him, and slipped her hand in Cam's. The bracelet fell to her wrist, and she felt something of that wildness that she had seen and loved in Cam and had wished to make part of herself. Now they faced the road together. The sun caught the silver clip in her hair and she knew that they had been joined together for years and years, for longer than either of them had lived or could even imagine.

They left the parkland and plunged into the woods that led to the road to the city. The Manor was out of sight now, and they were hidden by the trees. Cam stopped, picked a wild rose and wound it in Elaine's hair, working it through the silver clip of briars that had been his and was the second Jewel of Thorncliffe.

About the author

Judy Delaghty comes of a Travelling family and she had little formal education. When she was fourteen, she married in a traditional Travellers' Wedding. Her husband died just three weeks after the wedding, killed in a fight.

Judy still lives with her Travelling group and earns her living as a poet and storyteller. She has made contact with many other Travelling groups both in Europe and North America, and she is a leading authority on folk-tales of the Levant.

Valley of Wolves
by THERESA RADCLIFFE

CHAPTER I

THE TRAVELLER URGED his horse on. He was beginning to wish he'd not left the journey so late, or rather that he hadn't made it at all. The evening was closing in with alarming speed. The heavy clouds and biting wind could mean only one thing – snow was coming. The road through the mountains was flanked on either side by dark forests of fir and spruce. Even in daylight it was a sombre, forbidding place. Now, as dusk descended, it was the last place on earth the young lawyer wanted to find himself.

He was heading for the monastery of St Cleux, which lay on a remote hillside beyond the mountains. It was not so much the abbot's urgent summons which had brought him out, but the anticipation of a handsome fee. Mysteriously untouched by the plague, this isolated monastery had prospered in recent years and could still pay well for his services. Elsewhere plague, famine and harsh winters had devastated the country, bringing poverty and starvation to many. Wolves had left the mountains and forests and come down to the valleys to ravage towns and villages, carrying off unguarded livestock and unwary children or travellers.

The lawyer came upon the carriage quite suddenly, as the road turned a bend. It lay on its side, half off the road. Only a cluster of pine trees had prevented it slipping down the steep ravine. Pulling his horse to an abrupt halt, the shocked traveller kept his seat. He was uncertain whether he'd come upon the scene of some real misfortune, or whether this was an ambush set by evil brigands. He brought his horse forward cautiously, keeping alert to any sounds or movements which might indicate a hidden assailant. But as he drew nearer, he saw the gilded lilies and ravens on the carriage door and recognized at once the crest of the de Guise family. This was undoubtedly the carriage of the Count himself. Some terrible accident must have overtaken the Count and Countess de Guise.

The wind had dropped and flakes of snow were beginning to fall. The forest was strangely silent. The only sounds the traveller could hear were his horse's laboured breathing and his own heart pounding. He gripped tightly to the reins. He desperately wanted to ride on, but knew he could not. He dismounted slowly, steeling himself against what he might find, trying to suppress the inexplicable anxiety that filled him. After all, the horses had gone, and this was surely a good sign. The unfortunate occupants, unable to right the carriage, would have surely ridden off to find help rather than spend a night on this dangerous, desolate highway.

The young lawyer could see nothing from the road side of the carriage. He moved slowly round, holding on to the chassis and wheels to prevent himself slipping down the bank. The Count, he knew it was the Count by his fine boots and clothing, was lying face down some way from the carriage. A servant was stretched out in a pool of blood close by. The Countess, wrapped in furs and fine ermine lay half in, half out of the carriage door, the wound on her neck like a ribbon of garnet against the white fur.

The lawyer stood very still, as though needing time to take in the terrible scene in front of him. Then came the first howl, long, slow and mournful, jerking him back into action, to thoughts of his own safety. Then another and another, a rising chorus echoing through the forest. Wolves! He stumbled back up the bank. His horse was already moving its head and pawing the ground in alarm. He knew he had to reach his horse before fresh howling broke out and the terrified animal took off without him.

He approached the horse slowly, whispering soothing words. He mounted. He wanted to fly, to tear down the mountain, away from this awful scene, away from the wolves. But the snow was falling steadily now and it was nearly dark. One stumble, one slip and he could be thrown. Keeping a tight rein, he set off at a careful, steady pace.

As they moved slowly down the mountain it seemed that the forest had come alive. Shadows were sliding between the trees. He could see the glimmer, the glint of flashing eyes, and lean, hungry shapes stealing through the pines, padding silently towards the carriage. Suddenly he could bear it no longer. Grasping the horse's neck and digging in his heels, the lawyer set off at full gallop down the mountainside . . .

Also in DARK ENCHANTMENT

Firespell

by LOUISE COOPER

When Lianne looks into the heart of the topaz, she discovers the man she is to fall in love with – and at the same time reawakens an old family curse. But is the handsome face that beckons her from within the jewel one of good or evil? Is he from this world or the next? And can Lianne's love ever win?

The Hounds of Winter

by LOUISE COOPER

Tavia's marriage to a handsome but mysterious aristocrat kindles her sister Jansie's jealousy – but it also awakens a sinister force. For, as the first snow falls, the hounds of winter are unleashed and danger closes in. Can Jansie save her sister and herself?

Also in **DARK ENCHANTMENT**

Kiss of the Vampire

by J. B. CALCHMAN

The ancient town of St Doves rarely welcomes strangers and the arrival of Alex Culler, tall, dark, mysterious and ageless, reawakens superstitions that should have been dead and buried. Why is it, when she could have anyone, Ella wants Alex? And why is it he seems to find her just as irresistible?

Also in DARK ENCHANTMENT

Valley of Wolves

by THERESA RADCLIFFE

Every winter the wolves come down
from the mountains in search of food.
Every winter Marie remembers how she
lost her father and Jean-Pierre, the boy
she loved. But now she has been told
Jean-Pierre has returned from the dead.
And now the howling of wolves comes
from inside the château.